Ulrich Renz · Marc Rc

# The Wild Swans

# Los cisnes salvajes

Bilingual picture book based on a fairy tale by

Hans Christian Andersen

Translation:

Ludwig Blohm, Pete Savill (English)

Marcos Canedo, Anouk Bödeker (Spanish)

Download audiobook at:

www.sefa-bilingual.com/mp3

Password for free access:

English: **WSEN1423**

Spanish: **WSES1428**

Once upon a time there were twelve royal children –
eleven brothers and one older sister, Elisa. They lived
happily in a beautiful castle.

Había una vez doce hijos de un rey – once hermanos y
una hermana mayor, Elisa. Ellos vivían felices en un
castillo hermoso.

One day the mother died, and some time later the king married again. The new wife, however, was an evil witch. She turned the eleven princes into swans and sent them far away to a distant land beyond the large forest.

Un día murió la madre y algún tiempo después, el rey se volvió a casar. Pero la nueva esposa era una bruja malvada. Convirtió a los once principes en cisnes y les mandó a un país muy lejano más allá del gran bosque.

She dressed the girl in rags and smeared an ointment onto her face that turned her so ugly, that even her own father no longer recognized her and chased her out of the castle. Elisa ran into the dark forest.

A la niña la vistió con harapos y le puso una crema fea en la cara, de manera que ni su propio padre la reconoció y la echó del castillo. Elisa corrió al bosque oscuro.

Now she was all alone, and longed for her missing brothers from the depths of her soul. As the evening came, she made herself a bed of moss under the trees.

Ahora estaba más sola que nunca y añoró con toda el alma a sus hermanitos desaparecidos. Cuando anocheció, se hizo una cama de musgo bajo los árboles.

The next morning she came to a calm lake and was shocked when she saw her reflection in it. But once she had washed, she was the most beautiful princess under the sun.

Al día siguiente llegó a un lago de aguas tranquilas y se asustó cuando vió su imagen reflejada en el agua. Pero después de haberse lavado, fue la princesa más linda bajo el sol.

After many days Elisa reached the great sea. Eleven swan feathers were bobbing on the waves.

Después de muchos días, Elisa llegó al gran mar. En las olas, once plumas de cisne se mecían.

As the sun set, there was a swooshing noise in the air and eleven wild swans landed on the water. Elisa immediately recognized her enchanted brothers. They spoke swan language and because of this she could not understand them.

Cuando se puso el sol, hubo un murmullo en el aire y once cisnes salvajes aterrizaron sobre el agua. Elisa reconoció inmediatamente a sus hermanos embrujados. Pero como hablaban el idioma de cisnes, ella no les podía entender.

During the day the swans flew away, and at night the siblings snuggled up together in a cave.

One night Elisa had a strange dream: Her mother told her how she could release her brothers from the spell. She should knit shirts from stinging nettles and throw one over each of the swans. Until then, however, she was not allowed to speak a word, or else her brothers would die.
Elisa set to work immediately. Although her hands were burning as if they were on fire, she carried on knitting tirelessly.

De día los cisnes salían volando, de noche los hermanos y la hermana se acurrucaban el uno con el otro en una cueva.

Una noche, Elisa tuvo un sueño extraño: Su madre le dijo cómo podía liberar a sus hermanos. Tenía que tejer una camiseta de ortiga, una mala hierba con hojas punzantes, para cada uno de los cisnes y vestirles con ella. Pero hasta entonces no podía decir ni una palabra, de lo contrario sus hermanos morirían.
Elisa empezó de inmediato con su trabajo. Aunque sus manos le ardían como fuego, seguía tejiendo incansablemente.

One day hunting horns sounded in the distance. A prince came riding along with his entourage and he soon stood in front of her. As they looked into each other's eyes, they fell in love.

Un día sonaron cornetas de caza a lo lejos. Un principe llegó con su séquito y de pronto estuvo frente a ella. Cuando los dos se miraron a los ojos, se enamoraron.

The prince lifted Elisa onto his horse and rode to his castle with her.

El príncipe levantó a Elisa en su caballo y cabalgó con ella hasta su castillo.

The mighty treasurer was anything but pleased with the arrival of the silent beauty. His own daughter was meant to become the prince's bride.

El poderoso tesorero estaba de todo menos contento con la llegada de la bella princesa silenciosa. Pues su propia hija debía ser la novia del principe.

Elisa had not forgotten her brothers. Every evening she continued working on the shirts. One night she went out to the cemetery to gather fresh nettles. While doing so she was secretly watched by the treasurer.

Elisa no había olvidado a sus hermanitos. Cada noche seguía trabajando en las camisetas. Una noche se fue al cementerio para buscar ortigas frescas. En esto, el tesorero le observó en secreto.

As soon as the prince was away on a hunting trip, the treasurer had Elisa thrown into the dungeon. He claimed that she was a witch who met with other witches at night.

Tan pronto como el principe fue de cacería, el tesorero hizo meter en el calabozo a Elisa. Afirmó que era una bruja que se reunía con otras brujas por las noches.

At dawn, Elisa was fetched by the guards. She was going to be burned to death at the marketplace.

En la madrugada, Elisa fue recogida por los guardias. Debía ser quemada en la plaza principal.

No sooner had she arrived there, when suddenly eleven white swans came flying towards her. Elisa quickly threw a shirt over each of them. Shortly thereafter all her brothers stood before her in human form. Only the smallest, whose shirt had not been quite finished, still had a wing in place of one arm.

En cuanto llegó ahí, once cisnes blancos se acercaron
volando. Rápidamente Elisa les lanzó las camisetas
vistiendolos. De pronto todos sus hermanos se encontraban
frente a ella en su forma humana. Solo el menor, cuya
camiseta no estaba del todo terminada, se quedó con una ala
en lugar de un brazo.

The siblings' joyous hugging and kissing hadn't yet finished as the prince returned. At last Elisa could explain everything to him. The prince had the evil treasurer thrown into the dungeon. And after that the wedding was celebrated for seven days.

And they all lived happily ever after.

Las caricias y besos todavía no habían acabado cuando el principe regresó. Por fin Elisa le pudo explicar todo. El principe hizo meter en el calabozo al malvado tesorero. Y luego, se celebró la boda por siete días.

Y vivieron felices y comieron perdices.

# Hans Christian Andersen

Hans Christian Andersen was born in the Danish city of Odense in 1805, and died in 1875 in Copenhagen. He gained world fame with his literary fairy-tales such as „The Little Mermaid", „The Emperor's New Clothes" and „The Ugly Duckling". The tale at hand, „The Wild Swans", was first published in 1838. It has been translated into more than one hundred languages and adapted for a wide range of media including theater, film and musical.

# Marc Robitzky

Marc Robitzky, born in 1973, studied at the Technical School of Art in Hamburg and the Academy of Visual Arts in Frankfurt. He works as a freelance illustrator and communication designer in Aschaffenburg (Germany).

www.robitzky.eu

# Do you like drawing?

Here are the pictures from the story to color in:

# www.sefa-bilingual.com/coloring

## Enjoy!

## Dear Reader,

Thanks for choosing my book! If you (and most of all, your child) liked it, please spread the word via a Facebook-Like or an email to your friends:

www.sefa-bilingual.com/like

I would also be happy to get a comment or a review. Likes and comments are great TLC for authors, thanks so much!

If there is no audiobook version in your language yet, please be patient! We are working on making all the languages available as audiobooks. You can check the „Language Wizard" for the latest updates:

**www.sefa-bilingual.com/languages**

Now let me briefly introduce myself: I was born in Stuttgart in 1960, together with my twin brother Herbert (who also became a writer). I studied French literature and a couple of languages in Paris, then medicine in Lübeck. However, my career as a doctor was brief because I soon discovered books: medical books at first, for which I was an editor and a publisher, and later non-fiction and children's books.

I live with my wife Kirsten in Lübeck in the very north of Germany; together we have three (now grown) children, a dog, two cats, and a little publishing house: Sefa Press.

If you want to know more about me, you are welcome to visit my website: **www.ulrichrenz.de**

**Best regards,**

**Ulrich Renz**

# The wild swans also propose:

**Sleep Tight, Little Wolf**

**Que duermas bien, pequeño lobo**

Ulrich Renz / Barbara Brinkmann

English          bilingual          Spanish

Tim can't fall asleep. His little wolf is missing! Perhaps he forgot him outside?
Tim heads out all alone into the night – and unexpectedly encounters some friends ...

**Available in your languages?**

► Check out with our „Language Wizard":

**www.sefa-bilingual.com/languages**

Lulu can't fall asleep. All her cuddly toys are dreaming already – the shark, the elephant, the little mouse, the dragon, the kangaroo, and the lion cub. Even the bear has trouble keeping his eyes open ...
Hey bear, will you take me along into your dream?
Thus begins a journey for Lulu that leads her through the dreams of her cuddly toys – and finally to her own most beautiful dream.

**Available in your languages?**

► Check out with our „Language Wizard":

**www.sefa-bilingual.com/languages**

# More of me ...

# Bo & Friends

► Children's detective series in three volumes.  Reading age: 9+

► German Edition: „Motte & Co"  ► www.motte-und-co.de

► Download the series' first volume, „Bo and the Blackmailers" for free!

# www.bo-and-friends.com/free

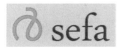

IT: Paul Bödeker, Freiburg, Germany

ISBN: 9783739958972

Version: 20190101

**www.sefa-bilingual.com**